MOONCAKE

A MOONBEAR Book

▪ FRANK ASCH ▪

ALADDIN

NEW YORK   LONDON   TORONTO   SYDNEY   NEW DELHI

ALADDIN

An imprint of Simon & Schuster Children's Publishing Division

1230 Avenue of the Americas, New York, NY 10020

This Aladdin edition March 2014

Copyright © 1983 by Frank Asch

For information about special discounts for bulk purchases, please contact

Simon & Schuster Special Sales at 1-866-506-1949 or business@simonandschuster.com.

The Simon & Schuster Speakers Bureau can bring authors to your live event.

For more information or to book an event contact the Simon & Schuster Speakers Bureau

at 1-866-248-3049 or visit our website at www.simonspeakers.com.

Designed by Karina Granda and Karin Paprocki

The text of this book was set in Olympian LT Std.

Manufactured China 1213 SCP

10 9 8 7 6 5 4 3 2 1

The Library of Congress has cataloged a previous edition as follows:

Asch, Frank. Mooncake

Summary: Bear builds a rocket to take him to the moon so he can taste it.

[1. Bears—Fiction. 2. Moon—Fiction.] I. Title

[PZ7. A778Mpd 1988] [E] 88-6571

ISBN 978-1-4424-9404-6 (hc)

ISBN 978-1-4424-9403-9 (pbk)

ISBN 978-1-4424-9405-3 (eBook)

To Devin
and the Cascos

One summer night Bear and his friend Little Bird sat down to watch the moon.

After a while Little Bird said: "I think I feel hungry."

"Me too," replied Bear. "And you know what I wish? I wish I could just jump up and take a bite out of the moon. Mmmmmmm, how delicious that would be!"

"How do you know?" chirped Little Bird. "Maybe the moon doesn't taste good at all. Maybe it tastes terrible!"

Bear thought for a moment.

Then he went inside and got his bow and arrow. With a piece of string, he attached a spoon to the arrow.

Then he went outside again

and shot the spoon at the moon.

"I knew that wouldn't work," said Little Bird. "The moon is just too far away. What you need is a rocket ship."

"Then I shall build one!" said Bear.

The very next day Bear went to the junkyard and bought everything he thought he would need to build a rocket ship.

All summer long Bear and Little Bird worked and worked, but when fall came, the rocket ship was still not finished.

"I would like to go with you," said Little Bird, "but winter is coming, and I must fly south with the flock."

So Bear and Little Bird said goodbye.

When it began to get cold and the leaves fell off the trees, Bear got sleepy. But instead of climbing into bed and

sleeping through the winter, he kept right on working. He worked and worked until the rocket ship was finished.

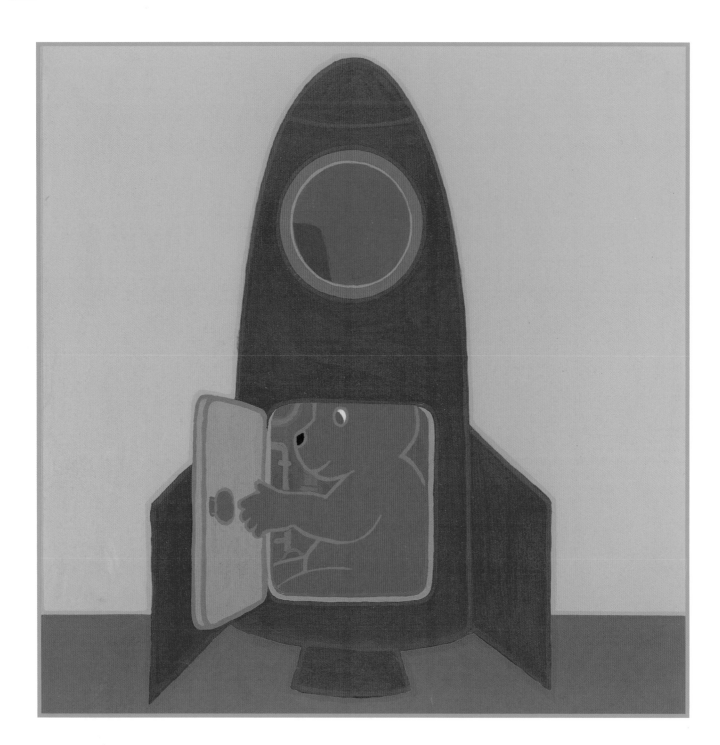

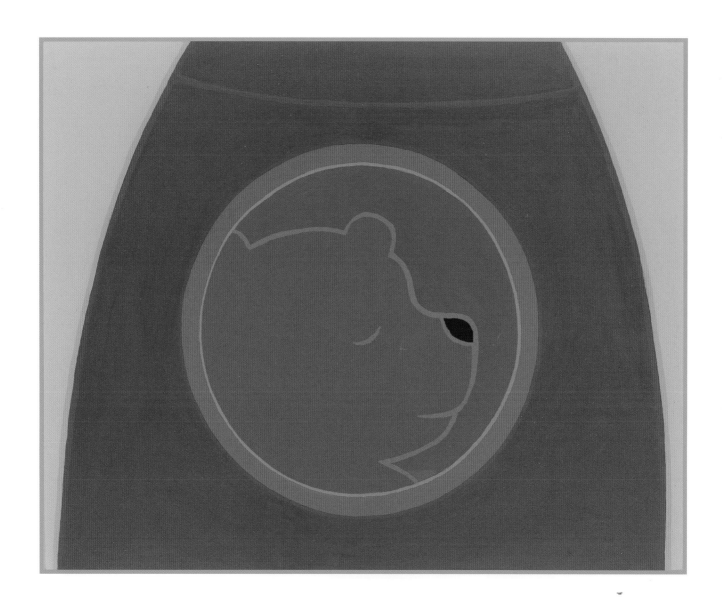

Then he climbed inside and began the countdown:
"10 9 8 7 6 5 4 3 2 zzzzzzz . . ."

But before he reached 1, he fell asleep.

He slept and slept and slept,

until one night the wind knocked over his rocket ship.

Bear had never been awake in the winter before. When he opened his eyes and saw all the snow, he thought he was on the moon.

He climbed out of his rocket ship, scooped up some snow, and made a little mooncake.

Then he tasted it.

It tasted like something he had tasted before, but he wasn't quite sure what it was.

While he thought about that, he decided to go for a walk.

He didn't want to go too far, because he was afraid that he would get lost. So he just walked in big circle.

After a while he came upon his own paw prints in the snow.

These paw prints are too big to belong to a moon mouse, or even a moon raccoon, thought Bear. *Maybe they were made by a moon bear, or perhaps*, he shuddered, *a terrible moon monster!*

Bear felt scared.

He ran back to his rocket ship and prepared for takeoff.

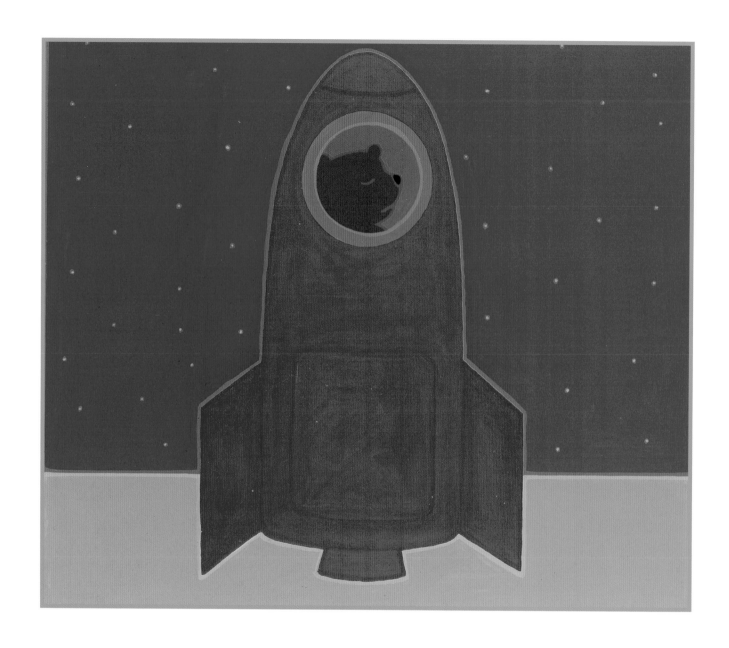

Again he began the countdown: "10 9 8 7 6 5 4 3 2 zzzz . . .," and again he fell asleep.

This time he slept until spring.

One day his friend Little Bird returned and woke him up.

"How was everything down south?" asked Bear.

"Just fine," said Little Bird.

"Did you go to the moon?" asked Little Bird.

"I sure did!" said Bear.

"And how did the moon taste?" asked Little Bird. "Was it terrible?"

"No," replied Bear, "it was delicious."